Lanie

by
Jane Kurtz

☆ American Girl®

For Ellemae and Noh, new to this world
of worm watching and ladybug loving

Published by American Girl Publishing, Inc.
Copyright © 2010 by American Girl, LLC

Questions or comments? Call 1-800-845-0005, visit our Web site at americangirl.com, or write to Customer Service, American Girl, 8400 Fairway Place, Middleton, WI 53562-0497.

Printed in China
10 11 12 13 14 15 LEO 10 9 8 7 6 5 4 3 2 1

Illustrations by Robert Papp; spot art by Rebecca DeKuiper

Special thanks to Kathe Crowley Conn

Cataloguing-in-Publication Data available from the Library of Congress.

Contents

On Friday, I ran home from school so fast, my little sister Emily could barely keep up with me. Our backpacks flapped behind us. This was the day I was going to test my best-ever scientific experiment.

As we burst through the door, Mom looked up from her desk. Before she could even say hello, Emily announced, "Stripey was munching and munching the milkweed leaves today."

Stripey is a monarch caterpillar. He lives in a big glass terrarium in Emily's first-grade classroom. I'm the fourth-grade helper in her class this month, so every morning I bring milkweed from the office refrigerator to Emily's classroom for the caterpillars to eat. Stripey is the biggest caterpillar in the cage, and he's our favorite. I always try to give him the juiciest-looking leaves.

Mom pulled us over for a hug. "So you were brave enough to watch Stripey today?" she asked Emily.

"Nope, but Lanie told me about it. She told me Stripey was munching something else, too!" Emily paused dramatically.

"What was it?" Mom asked, looking intrigued.

"His skin," I said quickly. Emily shouldn't get to tell *all* the news.

Factoid

As a caterpillar gets bigger, it
sheds its skin and eats it for
extra protein.

Dad stuck his head around the kitchen door.
"Speaking of munching, who's ready for this Friday's
spectacular snack?"

Emily and I looked at each other. Sometimes
Dad's spectacular Friday snacks are delicious. Sometimes . . . well . . . three words: corn ice cream.

"What is it, Dad?" asked Emily.

"Hopefully not caterpillar skin," I added.

Today's snack turned out to be homemade hum-
mus on pita bread arranged to look like slices of pizza,
since pizza is the only thing that Emily will eat, besides
dessert. My seven-year-old sister is very stubborn.
Once she decides something, she sticks to it—there's no
changing her mind. Fortunately, Dad loves cooking
challenges. A few months ago, he and I ran a secret
experiment to see how many foods we could get Emily
to eat.

The hypothesis: If it looks like pizza and we call

it pizza, Emily will eat it (usually). So Dad started serving every meal in pizza form: something flat and round on the bottom, with some kind of sauce or cheese spread over it, and little bits of food for the toppings. You'd be amazed how many different foods can be made to look like pizza.

The result: Emily ate everything but the rice-and-teriyaki-chicken pizza, which even she could tell wasn't really pizza.

Pizza isn't the only thing Emily is stubborn about. Ever since she found a spider in the sink once when she was brushing her teeth, she has been afraid of all bugs, even cute caterpillars like Stripey. She says bugs are too crawly and give her the creeps. Even though spring is finally here and the weather is turning nice, she won't go out into the yard to play because she's afraid of seeing a bug. Normally I wouldn't care, but ever since my best friend, Dakota, left, Emily is about the only person I have around here to play with after school.

In fact, I've recently made a discovery about my family: Nobody likes being outdoors very much except me. I think it's because Mom, Dad, and my two sisters were born with inside genes, and I was born with outside genes. The genetic mismatch must have happened before I was born, when I was still gestating inside my mother.

I did research on gestation periods when I was waiting for Dakota's lop-eared rabbit to have babies. Thirty-one days may not seem like much, but since one of the baby bunnies was going to become my first pet, it didn't seem short to me at all. Almost every day I told Dakota, "This is taking forever!"

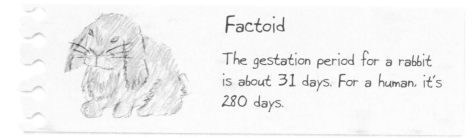

Factoid

The gestation period for a rabbit is about 31 days. For a human, it's 280 days.

My rabbit, Lulu, has turned out to be the best pet ever and definitely worth waiting for. She was also about to become the subject of my best-ever scientific experiment.

I finished my snack, climbed the two flights of stairs to my room, which is at the very tip-top of our house, and unhooked the door to Lulu's pen. I took her walking vest down from a hook as she hopped over to see me.

The Bunny Experiment

Not all rabbits like to go for walks. When I e-mailed Dakota to tell her what I was planning, she had warned me it might not work. Luckily, I am a scientist. And scientists always learn from experiments, whether they succeed or fail. After four careful steps and a *lot* of work, this was the day when I'd know for sure—would my experiment be a success?

Step One. I spent hours lying on the floor and letting Lulu sniff me, hop on me, and eat vegetables and alfalfa pellets out of my hand.

Step Two. When Lulu completely trusted me, I put the walking vest on her for a few minutes. Every day she wore it a little longer.

Step Three. I clipped a leash to the vest and let her lead me around my bedroom so we could both get the feel of the leash.

Step Four. I took her out into our backyard. The very first time she was outside, she stood absolutely still for a minute, with only her nose twitching. Then she leaped high in the air and kicked her legs in a joyful rabbit dance. That's when I knew she must have outside genes, too.

Today, as I buckled Lulu into her vest, I felt a bit nervous. What if my experiment didn't work? For Lulu's sake I tried to act calm as I picked her up and put her inside what I like to call the bunny elevator.

Mom's an architect, and when I was little she completely redesigned the inside of our house. It's on a narrow lot, but it's tall—three stories high, with lots of big windows and little decks so that it sort of feels like living in a tree house. Because of the height, Mom added some special devices for convenience. We have an open metal staircase with a long open shaft down the middle, so she put in a dumbwaiter. It's like a miniature elevator, with a platform and walls made of recycled plywood, slightly larger than a laundry basket. That's the main thing Mom uses it for—hauling dirty laundry downstairs to the washing machine and clean laundry back upstairs to the bedrooms. But I discovered it makes a perfect bunny elevator. You just press a button, and the gears silently turn a long chain—Mom says she used bicycle technology—and down goes the elevator with Lulu in it.

I zipped downstairs to meet her. I lifted her out and carried her to the front porch and set her down. Lulu's nose went *wiggle, wiggle, wiggle*. Then she hopped right down our front walk to the sidewalk.

Thrilldom!

Walking a rabbit isn't like walking a dog. Rabbits won't follow you; you have to follow them. I strolled behind Lulu, holding the leash loosely, and we gradually made our way down the sidewalk.

We were the biggest show on the block. Our neighbor in the gray house, Mr. Werlin, stopped clipping his hedge and stared when we went by his yard. The nanny of the twins in the next house pulled their double stroller to the edge of the sidewalk so we could go by, and the twins leaned over their trays to watch Lulu nip some clover. As we passed Professor Kosko, who is retired and likes to read on her porch, she looked over the top of her glasses and called, "That little vest makes your friend look like Peter Rabbit."

Sadly, Lulu can never have a Peter Rabbit adventure, because our block doesn't have any vegetable gardens for her to sneak into—just squares of green grass, all down the block. But she does like vegetables, so I was using bits of carrot to coax her along.

We went down to the end of the street and turned around and headed back. I was thrilled: My rabbit-walking experiment was a big success! Now I could take Lulu out for walks every day after school. Who cared if Emily wouldn't come out with me? I had my faithful bunny for company. As we headed back up the street to our house, I started to dream about being a real animal scientist someday. . . .

The Bunny Experiment

. . . It's dawn in the mountains of Mongolia, and I'm making my way carefully along a steep mountain trail, hoping to spot a snow leopard. They're super shy and super well camouflaged—only the sharpest eyes can spot them. Suddenly, I see movement ahead— Can it be?—Yes, a furry, twitching tail . . .

Wait a minute. Since when did our new next-door neighbor get a cat?

I stopped. A large orange cat sat hunched in the driveway of the house next door, staring at Lulu with big green eyes. The cat arched its back and hissed. Lulu froze. The cat hissed louder. Then suddenly Lulu did the exact opposite of what I would have predicted.

She charged the cat.

I was so surprised, I dropped the leash. The cat yowled and dashed away from Lulu. As I scrambled for the leash, a door slammed and our new neighbor came running down her front walk in high heels, shouting, "Get control of that rabbit!"

I grabbed Lulu's leash and picked her up. She was trembling. I stroked her and let her bury her head inside the curve of my arm.

The lady cleared her throat and looked at me. "I'm Ms. Marshall. I don't think we've met yet. I just moved in next door."

"I'm Lanie," I mumbled.

"Do you walk your rabbit often?" Ms. Marshall asked.

"Um, well, this is actually the first time I've ever tried it," I told her.

"Perhaps it should be the last time, too," she said. "This is the first time *I've* let Caesar out of our new house, and now he's totally traumatized. It's hard enough for a cat to adjust to a new home, without being attacked by a vicious rodent."

Lulu, a vicious rodent? Wrong on both counts.

"Rabbits aren't rodents," I said.

She snorted and gave me a tiny little superior smile. "Of course they are."

It was obvious she thought I was just a dumb kid who didn't know anything about anything. She didn't realize she was dealing with a scientist.

I drew myself up to my full height of four feet nine inches. "Rabbits are lagomorphs, not rodents,"

I informed her. "You can look it up if you don't believe me."

That little factoid made her pause. Then she shrugged and said, "Well, whatever your rabbit is, do me a favor and please keep it away from my cat." She turned and marched back up her front walk, her high heels going *click, click, click.* I headed glumly across our front lawn and went inside.

I'm usually the first one awake in my family. House sounds tend to carry up our open stairwell, and since my room is right at the top of the stairs, I can hear everything. That might bother some people, but I like it. Sometimes in the morning I lie in bed pretending to be a wildlife tracker, listening to each sound and seeing how long it takes me to identify who's making it. As soon as I hear any noise in the house, I start counting inside my head. *One-one-hundred, two-one-hundred, three-one-hundred . . .* This morning I didn't even get to ten before I heard the first cello notes.

That's my big sister, Angela. She's sixteen and her life ambition is to be a concert cellist, so the first thing she does each morning, even before she brushes her teeth, is practice her cello. She's been working on the *William Tell* Overture. I used to really like that piece, but hearing it a few hundred times is kind of like wearing an itchy wool sweater in the summer. Irritating!

Faint clanking from down in the kitchen—that would be Mom. She likes to make breakfast for everyone on the weekends. Her pineapple pancakes are to die for.

Thwock, thwock, thwock! That can be only one

person—Dad, out on the back deck batting a paddle ball. You know, one of those rubber balls attached to a wooden paddle with an elastic string. It might seem goofy—Angela has made him promise not to do it when her friends are around—but he claims that mindless repetition helps him think.

My dad's a professional thinker. "Your mother's job earns money for the mortgage," he says when we tease him about the paddle ball. "Mine funds the fun, so I recommend that you let me think." Actually, he teaches philosophy to college students.

Inside a lecture hall.

And his hobby is cooking. *Inside* the kitchen. In fact, about the only time he goes outside is to pound the paddle ball.

With a sigh, I got out of bed and flopped down flat on the floor by Lulu to see how she was doing after yesterday's cat disaster.

She wiggled her nose at me. The more interested she is in something, the quicker her nose wiggles. *I'm fascinated,* her nose seemed to be saying. *What's wrong?*

Well, for one thing, I'm surrounded by people who don't care if they sit inside until they're as pale as Kentucky cave shrimp.

Factoid

Kentucky cave shrimp never leave their caves or see the sunlight. They feed on tiny bits of stuff that seep into their river caves from groundwater.

And for another thing, I really miss Dakota.

Dakota and I have been best friends since kindergarten, but fourth grade was going to be our best year ever. On our first day of school last fall, our teacher, Mr. James, had looked over the top of his glasses, given us all a huge smile, and said, "Welcome, fellow explorers of the wide, wonderful world."

Dakota leaned over and whispered, "Ooh-la-la!" That was the moment we knew we were going to love fourth grade, because we were both born to be explorers.

Dakota and I want to be wildlife biologists when we grow up. We often talk about what kinds of animals we want to study—the more exotic, the better. We might track elephants as they rumble across the savannah, or follow in the footsteps of our idol, Jane Goodall, and study chimpanzees.

Then, halfway through fourth grade, Dakota's family moved away. And not just across the city or even to another state—they moved to the other side of the planet, to Indonesia. Her dad's a professor of forestry, and he wanted to study the Indonesian rain forests, so off they went. Mom keeps reminding me that it's only for six months and they'll be back as soon as school is out, but it feels like forever. So now Dakota and I have to talk to each other by e-mail.

In her first e-mails from Indonesia, Dakota told me all about her new school (tiny), the swimming pool near her house (huge), and her new friends (not as great as I am). About the only new thing I had to write about was Stripey the caterpillar. I told Dakota how all he eats is milkweed, which is very bitter and in fact toxic to most animals, but not to monarch caterpillars. That's why birds won't eat monarch butterflies—they taste bitter and make the birds sick, because of all the milkweed they ate when they were caterpillars. Dakota thought that was interesting.

Well, at least now I had something exciting to tell Dakota about—the results of my bunny-walking experiment and the mean cat lady next door. I got up and went over to my desk and switched on my laptop.

A message popped up: *You have mail!*

From: "Dakota" <dakotanotthestate@4natr.net>
Date: April 16, 2010 4:42 P.M.
To: "Lanie" <hollandnotthecountry@4natr.net>
Subject: Wait till you hear this!

Guess what? My school, which is right at the edge of the rain forest, has a program for kids to volunteer at--get this--an orangutan conservation center! It's a few miles away, inside the rain forest, and it's really cool. There are large enclosed habitats for orangutans who have been injured or orphaned or just displaced by logging in the forest. The center takes them in and treats their injuries and helps them recover, and then releases them.

This week we got to tour the center and watch the orangutans. They're amazing animals. Did you know they're smart enough to use big leaves as umbrellas? (It rains a lot here!) We get to go back again tomorrow and actually help out. I can't wait. I'm going to be a wildlife researcher, Lanie--just like we always talked about. Thrilldom!

Wow. I was speechless.

I knew what Mr. James would say: "When you're feeling uncertain, try capturing a few thoughts as they flap by and test them out. That's what scientists do."

I closed my eyes, reached into my brain, and

captured a thought. Actually, it was more of a feeling.
I tested it out. Was it a warm, friendly, fizzy feeling, the
kind I usually get when I hear from Dakota?

No, it was different. Was it an excited, I'm-so-
happy-you're-living-your-dreams feeling? No, it wasn't
that either.

It was an icky, sickly feeling.

I even knew its name.

Envy.

The intercom in my bedroom buzzed, jolting me
out of my thoughts. The intercom is another of Mom's
convenience inventions, but she's the only one who
actually uses it. I pushed the button. "Hi, Mom."

"Pancakes are ready!" Her voice flew into my
room. "Hurry down—I have some exciting news."

I'd already had all the exciting news I could
handle for one morning (*more* than I could handle,
to be honest), but I didn't tell her that. I switched
off my laptop, threw on some clothes, and headed
downstairs.

When we were all gathered at the table passing
the pancakes and maple syrup, Mom announced,

"Guess what? Your Aunt Hannah just called, and she's coming to visit!"

We all cheered. Emily jumped up and started hopping on one foot as she clapped. Even I cheered, despite my mood. Aunt Hannah is Mom's adventurous younger sister. She's always doing something amazing, such as climbing trees to study rare birds in Hawaii. Someday, I'm going to have incredible adventures just like her.

Mom was suddenly all business. "Emily, please stop jumping around, and go get the shopping list from the refrigerator. Angela, can you clean up the breakfast things while I get the guest bed ready? Hannah said she'd be here by dinnertime, so we have lots to do."

Dad stood up. "That's a great excuse to make my Australian ginger fish. Lanie, want to go shopping with me?"

I grabbed the cloth shopping bags we keep by the back door. "I'm ready."

"Can I come too?" Emily asked.

Tell her no. I tried to send the thought to Dad using telepathy. Emily is so annoying to shop with— she has to look at every single thing in the store, and always wants to buy stuff she'll never eat, just because she likes the picture on the box.

"Not this time, sweetie," he said. "Lanie's my assistant today."

I thanked Dad by telepathy, grabbed my jacket, and followed him outside. Still, I felt a tiny bit bad as I saw Emily's face smooshed against the window.

"Looks like the lawn needs mowing again already," Dad murmured. "Gosh, but it grows fast in the spring. People may complain about our Boston winters, but I tell you, I don't miss mowing the lawn. Maybe this year I could just skip it and let it go natural."

I looked at the grass. He was right. It was getting long, and dandelion heads had already popped up. Compared to the lawns on either side of us, ours looked shaggy and messy.

"But Dad, if you don't mow it, our yard will look bad," I pointed out. "Besides, don't you love the smell of fresh-cut grass?"

He smiled. "You're right, honey. Maybe if we hurry, I can get to it this afternoon, before Hannah arrives."

Dad looked at his grocery list. "We need cheese—mozzarella and a chunk of Parmesan. Are you on it?"

Of course I was on it. I closed my eyes and let my nose guide me past the produce aisle toward the cheese counter. In science, Mr. James had told us how lots of animals map their world by smell, not vision. They rely on different smells to tell them where they are and what's nearby—food, water, friends, enemies— just the way we humans rely on sight and sound.

I kept my eyes closed, trying to catch the cool, tart aroma of the cheese counter. Could I make it the rest of the way by smell alone? I inched forward . . .

> . . . *I'm a rare Indian rhinoceros, making my way through the tall grass where I feed at night. Like all rhinos, I prefer to be solitary. My eyesight is lousy, but that doesn't matter because I have an awesome sense of smell. And besides, nobody messes with me! I trudge along—*

"Hey." A little boy's raspy voice broke in. "What are you doing? Are you blind?"

My eyes flew open. "Um, no, I'm—never mind." I hurried to the cheese counter, grabbed a mozzarella ball and a wedge of Parmesan, and zipped back to Dad.

"I think we're done here," Dad said as he steered the cart to the checkout line. "Let's go to the Spice Route next. I need some Australian ginger, and you can choose something for dessert."

I leaned against him, feeling a little down. I knew Dad expected me to be delighted. Going to the Spice Route, with its exotic smells and drumming music and brightly patterned silks hanging from the ceiling, had always seemed exciting, like exploring a foreign country. But now, when I compare it to helping save orangutans in Indonesia . . .

"Lanie? You okay?"

I shrugged.

Dad narrowed his eyes at me. "I'm switching on my telepathic mind-reading mental powers. I'm seeing a fourth-grader . . . she has green hair . . . no, wait, that's her eye color." I giggled as Dad went on. "She's a little bit . . . lonely. Her best friend is . . . far, far away, having grand adventures in a fabulous place, and she's left behind . . . the picture is fading . . ." He opened his eyes, and I gave him a hug. Sometimes Dad sure knows how to put two and two together.

One thing was for certain. Just because I lived with a bunch of Kentucky cave shrimp didn't mean I had to be one. What I needed were some *real* adventures.

After lunch, I rallied myself and e-mailed Dakota a reply. I told her how good Lulu was on our walk and how she had bravely fought off a skilled predator, *Felis domesticus*. That's the scientific name for the house cat. I knew Dakota would know that and would appreciate being talked to as one scientist to another. I also told her about *Homo sapiens horribilis*, a.k.a. Ms. Marshall.

It seemed too cruel to keep Lulu inside on such a sunny afternoon, so when I was done on the computer, I took her out onto my bedroom deck. Our house has four little private decks, one off each bedroom, and one big one off the kitchen and living room. They're all made of recycled milk jugs that have been squished up and turned into plastic lumber. From my deck on the third floor, it's really like being in a tree house. I can see our whole backyard.

Setting Lulu down, I plopped into the hanging chair and opened my private notebook. I turned to a fresh page and wrote at the top:

Real Adventures!
Step One:
Convince Mom & Dad to take us camping.

Hey, maybe Aunt Hannah could be helpful with that—she loves camping.

Before I could write anything else, I heard a
car pull into the driveway. Aunt Hannah was here!
I scrambled out of the chair and leaned over the deck
railing to wave at her—and stared at something
trundling along behind her car. Could it be? Yes!
Aunt Hannah was towing a camper. It was as if she
had read my mind. Maybe she
has mental telepathy like Dad
and me!

The car door opened,
and my aunt got out. I waved
my arms and called, and she
looked up, grinned, and gave
me a thumb's-up.

The side door banged open, and Emily leaped
down the stairs to fling herself at Aunt Hannah.
"What's that? Is that where you live?" she squealed.
Before Aunt Hannah could answer, Emily charged on.
"Did you know Dad made ginger fish for you, but
pizza for me?"

"Hi, Aunt Hannah." Angela's voice floated out
from her deck, which is just below mine.

Dad called from the kitchen window, "Congratu-
lations, Hannah, your timing is perfect—dinner's just
about ready."

Perfect indeed. Dinner would be the perfect time for me to announce Real Adventures, Step One.

I put Lulu back in her pen and hurried down two flights of stairs, wishing—not for the first time—that *I* could fit into the bunny elevator.

"Hey, Lanie!" Aunt Hannah said when she saw me. "Come here and hug me like you mean it."

That's what she always says. I ran to her, feeling both happy to see her and a little bit shy.

Emily was not the least bit shy. She tugged on Aunt Hannah's arm. "Dad put broccoli on the pizza. Do you like broccoli? I don't, but I eat it if it's on pizza. Will you eat it if it's on pizza?"

"Honey, I'm sure Aunt Hannah likes broccoli just fine," Mom laughed, squeezing in to give her sister a hug.

"The fish is done—let's eat!" Dad announced, and we all sat down at the table. All except for Angela, who was settling the spike of the cello into its holder.

Mom looked at Angela. "Wouldn't you like to wait and provide us with *after*-dinner music?"

"Nope," Angela said, arranging her music importantly. "This is an elegant meal with a special guest, and I'm providing the elegant *during*-dinner music." She drew her bow and began to play while we ate.

When everyone but Angela had eaten, Dad tapped on his glass. "Lanie personally selected the dessert delicacy we are about to enjoy." He handed me a plate that held the large chocolate bar I'd picked out earlier. "Lanie, you're on."

This was my chance—quickly now, while I had their attention. I stood up. I cleared my throat importantly. I held up the bar of chococate.

"The cocoa beans in this very chocolate bar came all the way from Mexico. In fact, the chocolate even comes with a map." I pointed to a picture on the back of the wrapper. "The map shows the exact journey the cocoa beans made from Mexico to Missouri to make the chocolate you're about to eat. You can even go to their Web site and follow the journey of the cocoa beans. Or—" I hesitated, then plunged ahead. "I think that if cocoa beans can go on a journey and have adventures, then our family can, too." I stretched out my arms in a *ta-da* way and made my big announcement. "I think we should all go camping!"

Aunt Hannah smiled. "Terrific idea!"

Angela played a low, groaning note on her cello. "Not."

"*I* think it's a good idea," Emily said loyally.

I gave her a grateful smile and sat down.

"You can't cook pizza when you're camping," Angela pointed out. She leaned her cello in the corner and helped herself to some salad. "But there are sure to be plenty of bugs."

Emily looked wide-eyed with concern.

Uh-oh. I started snapping the chocolate into pieces.

Angela pointed a piece of pizza at me. "Lanie, you're too young to remember our camping trip— or should I say camping *fiasco*." She turned to Dad. "Remember that place? Wasn't it called something dopey like Sherwood Forest?"

"Yes, and I *sure would* not go there again." Dad smirked at his own joke.

Angela grimaced. "I remember ants got into our box of cereal, and we had to lock all our garbage in the car so raccoons couldn't get it."

Mom looked amused at the memory. "And we didn't know about using a rain fly, so the rain started coming through the tent, and our sleeping bags got all wet and soggy. It *was* a pretty icky mess."

"I don't remember any of this," I said.

"You were just a baby, Lanie," Angela replied.

How cruel—I had gone camping and couldn't even remember it.

Lanie

Mom cleared her throat. "Of course, all that was before the *real* fiasco."

Dad smiled halfheartedly. "You mean when I stepped in that hole and broke my ankle?"

Mom made a face. "Your ankle—*and* our bank account, because of that exciting helicopter rescue."

"Face it, Lanie," said Angela as she snagged the last piece of ginger fish. "Camping just isn't our thing."

"But Aunt Hannah even has a camper now. It would be perfect." I felt like telling them they were all a bunch of wimpy cave shrimp, but I felt too deflated. I gave my piece of chocolate to Emily and slumped back down on my seat.

Aunt Hannah leaned over and gave me a squeeze. "I think it's a great idea. But it sounds like we're outvoted." Then she tapped on her water glass like Dad. "Here's the big news that goes along with my new camper," she said. "I'm moving back to Boston, because I'm going back to school."

Emily looked at her thoughtfully. "You're too old to go to school."

Aunt Hannah laughed. "It's never too late to learn more about the things you love. The camper will be my house and laboratory this summer until I can get university housing in the fall. Requesting permission to park in your driveway." She added, "I'll take care of the yard, and the girls and I can find adventures and fun things to do right here in Boston."

Everyone started talking at once. I cleared my plate and slipped upstairs. Once again, my brain was filled with confusing feelings flapping around.

I knew I should be thrilled that Aunt Hannah was going to be staying with us for the summer. And I was, truly. But for some reason, it didn't cheer me up. Maybe because I realized it did me no good that Aunt Hannah and I both got the same outside genes while we were gestating. In the Holland family, our genes were outnumbered *and* outvoted. Total woe.

Still, Aunt Hannah's announcement was news, which gave me an excuse to e-mail Dakota. When I turned on my laptop, I saw she had e-mailed me first.

From: Dakota <dakotanotthestate@4natr.net>
Date: April 17, 2010 10:02 P.M.
To: Lanie <hollandnotthecountry@4natr.net>
Subject: Wow!

I can't believe Lulu was brave enough to attack a cat! I'm impressed you got her to walk on the leash, too!

Today we went to the orangutan center and took field notes. We had to observe and write down everything that happened, just like Jane Goodall. It was a little bit sad, actually. Fio is a new orphaned young orangutan. They just put her in with some others, and she wants company, but the bigger orangutans keep pulling her hair and being mean to her. They were even baring their teeth at her. Finally she had to be put back into a cage by herself, but I could tell she wasn't happy there, either. She just sat in a corner and looked sad. I've attached a picture of her. Isn't she adorable?

I miss u tons & wish u were here. xox

The photo showed Dakota standing outside a fence, smiling for the camera. Inside the fence, a sweet little orangutan clung to a branch and looked out at me with sad brown eyes. I thought of the poor, lonely little orang- utan and wished with all my heart that there was some way I could help her.

Then I looked again at Dakota and thought of her over there in the rain forest in Indonesia, getting to study and help these amazing, adorable creatures.

The envy burned all the way down to my toes.

Monday morning, before the first bell, I made my milkweed delivery to Emily's classroom. Stripey looked pretty much the same as always, maybe a little bit bigger. He was kind of cute, with his bright yellow and black stripes.

Not as cute as Fio the orangutan, my brain whispered back at me, but I pushed the thought away and headed for Mr. James's classroom.

At my desk, I opened a library book about Jane Goodall. I read that when Jane was a girl, her family once called the police because she was missing. It turned out she'd been sitting in the henhouse for four hours trying to figure out how a hen lays an egg. At the time she started studying chimpanzees, she still didn't have formal scientific training. She just wrote down everything she saw. Field notes. Like the ones Dakota was taking at the orangutan center.

Dakota and I had always planned to be wildlife researchers together. Now she was getting to start without me.

I frowned. Maybe *I* should take field notes about something, too, just for practice.

Last week, Mr. James had shown us a video of scientists observing meerkats in their natural habitat in Africa. Mr. James said that the scientists study meerkats, which are very social and playful, to develop theories about why animals play. The meerkats were quite entertaining. In the video, they sometimes climbed up the scientists' backs and performed lookout duties standing on the scientists' shoulders or heads!

I took out a pencil and looked around for something to observe. Studying fourth-graders didn't seem nearly as fun or interesting as studying meerkats, but it was all I had to practice on.

The first bell rang. Mr. James opened the door, and all the fourth-graders rushed in. They didn't notice that I was observing them; they just acted the way they always do in their natural habitat.

"Guess what," Noah said to Max in a loud voice. "I saw Yuke homer at the Red Sox game on Saturday. I was *this close* to catching the ball."

Max shrugged. "Big deal."

Noah gave him a shove and pretended to bat a baseball.

Fourth-grade boy behaviors: loud voices, bragging, shoving, I wrote.

We start every Monday morning writing in our science journals. We can write about anything, as long as we are writing. In front of me, Kira was scribbling away like a meerkat digging in the dirt. Jeremy, on my left, looked like a meerkat in the video that had fallen asleep standing up and then toppled off the burrow. Jeremy's eyelids were drooping and he looked as if he might fall asleep on his desk. I started sketching a sleepy meerkat that looked like Jeremy.

Kira turned around and eyed my work. "I wish I could draw like you," she whispered.

I shrugged modestly. Drawing fourth-graders as meerkats was kind of fun, but I doubted it was as fascinating as observing real orangutans.

Kira whipped back around to her desk. "Better start writing," she muttered. "The chief meerkat's on the march." Mr. James was coming up the aisle, checking notebooks to be sure we were writing.

"Thanks!" I whispered, turning a page to begin a new entry in my journal.

Kira would make a good meerkat.

Factoid

Meerkats are excellent sentinels. They watch for danger and warn the others if it approaches.

The next day, Tuesday, was my day to be the
fourth-grade helper in Emily's room. When I arrived,
Emily bounced up and grabbed my hand. "The caterpillars are hanging this morning!" she exclaimed.

I hurried in to look. Several of the caterpillars
had made little silk buttons on the sticks in their cage
and were hanging from the buttons in curved J-shapes.
I wished Dakota were here to see it—she'd be fascinated.
I could almost hear her saying, "Ooh-la-la!"

The other first-graders kept stopping by to peek
into the terrarium. I was supposed to be helping them
with their math, but the teacher, Mrs. Kaminsky,
seemed to understand how exciting this was—for the
first-graders and for me—and let the math slide. But
Emily was still hanging back.

"Come on, Emily, you've got to see this," I
coaxed. "The ones that are hanging aren't crawly
at all anymore. At least come look at them."

"Is Stripey hanging?"

Now that the caterpillars were no longer
stretched out, it was impossible to tell for certain
which one was Stripey, but since he had been the
largest one, I felt pretty certain he would have been

among the first to start turning into a pupa.

"Yes, he is," I said. "Don't you want to see him?" Emily looked at the terrarium from halfway across the room. "It's your last chance to see him as a caterpillar, you know," I pointed out.

Finally, she approached and stood about three feet away, peering at the terrarium from behind my arm. "Which one is Stripey?"

"That one." I pointed to the largest hanging J.

"Cool," Emily breathed. "Hi, Stripey, how do you like hanging there? Is it fun?"

"He looks like he's having fun," I said. "See? He's wiggling all around." In fact, all of the caterpillars were twitching and squirming, shedding their skins like scrunched-up sleeping bags. Some of them had already started to form the bright green covering of the pupa, which we learned was called the chrysalis. It was one of the coolest things I'd ever seen.

"How long until they turn into butterflies?" Emily asked her teacher.

"They'll be pupas for about two weeks," said Mrs. Kaminsky. "By the time we all get back from spring break, the adult butterflies should be ready to emerge."

I asked Mrs. Kaminsky if I could go and get my

science journal. She nodded, so I hurried down the hall
and returned with my journal and my colored pencils.
Now I could *really* take some field notes.

As soon as Emily and I got home from school, we
went to knock on the door of Aunt Hannah's camper,
which was now parked just off the driveway in the
backyard.

"C'mon in!" Aunt Hannah called from inside.

As we stepped inside, Emily breathed, "Ooh!
It's a fairy house!"

I saw what she meant. It had regular house stuff,
but everything was small-sized and cozy and cleverly
fit together. There was a mini fridge, a tiny sink, and a
single-burner stove. Colorful nature posters were taped
to the walls and cabinets. At the table, Aunt Hannah
had her laptop open and books and papers spread out.
She was listening with headphones and making notes.

"Hi! What's up, girls?" she asked, taking off the
headphones.

I started to tell her, but I was no match for my
motormouth sister. "Our caterpillars started hanging
in J's! Mrs. Kaminsky said they probably started doing it

in the middle of the night when we were all asleep and we didn't know when they would start turning into pupils, so we should all keep our observating eyes open."

"Pupas," I said. "They'll turn into *pupas*. And *observating* isn't a word." I pulled out my journal and passed it to Aunt Hannah. I suddenly felt shy again, showing a real-life scientist my notes and drawings, but I wanted to see what she thought of them.

Emily draped herself over Aunt Hannah's shoulder as she paged through my field notes. "The caterpillars were wiggling and squiggling. I thought it was weird," Emily whispered loudly in Aunt Hannah's ear. "But Lanie said it was science."

"Weird science. My favorite!" Aunt Hannah laughed. Then she touched my drawing of a caterpillar. "These sketches are really good, Lanie. You're getting better and better as an artist." She looked up at me. "Where did you learn to take such good field notes?"

Emily took Aunt Hannah's head in her hands and turned it to face her. "The caterpillars are in *my* classroom, so *I'm* going to see them turn into pupils before Lanie does." She took my journal right out of Aunt Hannah's hands. "Lanie says she's going to use her colored pencils to draw what the pupil looks like. She said maybe I could help. Can I, Lanie?"

"No!" The word burst out. "And if you don't give me back my journal right now, I'm never letting you use my colored pencils, ever."

Aunt Hannah scooted back to her desk. "Hey, Emily, I have a notebook you can have that has hardly anything in it. Why don't you give Lanie her journal."

"Noooo!" Emily let out a wail. "I want Lanie's. She knows how to make pictures." She clutched my open journal with both hands. I reached for it, but she held on to it stubbornly, her fingers wrinkling the pages and smudging the pencil sketches.

"Stop!" I shouted, pointing to show her what she'd done. She looked horrified and quickly let go. Then she ran sobbing out of the trailer.

Sometimes when I get frustrated with Emily, Mom says to me, "Try to be generous. It isn't easy being a little sister. Ask Aunt Hannah about that some-time." But I know my aunt couldn't possibly have ever been *this* irritating.

As if she had been reading my thoughts, Aunt Hannah said, "Little sisters can be tough stuff. I know, because I'm a little sister too." She stood up and took my hand. "Come on, it's too nice a day to stay indoors."

I followed her out into the backyard. Something looked different. I pointed to a large pile of dirt at the end of the driveway. "Where did that come from?"

"I had some topsoil delivered this afternoon. I thought we could plant a vegetable garden. Maybe some wildflowers, too. What do you think?"

"Um . . . sure," I said uncertainly.

Out of the corner of my eye I saw something move in the yard next door. Caesar was prowling across the lawn super slowly, as if he was stalking some prey. When he saw me look at him, he froze and stared back at me with his green eyes. Then, suddenly, he sat down and began to lick his paws, as if to say, *See? I'm a totally innocent creature, just minding my own business.*

I glanced past him at Ms. Marshall's back terrace. Next to a curly white metal table were rows and rows of little boxes. There must have been twenty or thirty boxes, maybe more. The boxes had something in them, but I couldn't quite tell what. Spiky branches, it looked like. Odd.

"Lanie?" said a voice. A whiny voice. Emily.

Great—pests were multiplying. What did *she* want?

When I turned around, Emily was holding out a piece of paper. On it was a picture of Stripey, carefully colored in with crayons.

"See? I could help you." Emily scuffed her toe on

the deck. "Can I use your colored pencils and color some field notes in your journal?"

My heart softened—a little. "No, but I will let you use my sixty-four-color box of crayons, if you promise to be super-duper careful with them. You can use recycled paper from Dad." He brings home piles of used paper from his office for us, and we use the back sides to color on.

Emily's face lit up. "Can I color right out here on the deck with you and Aunt Hannah?"

"Sure." As I went in to get the crayons, it hit me: maybe I could coax the littlest Kentucky cave shrimp out of its cave.

When I returned to the deck, I told Emily, "Aunt Hannah and I are going to make a garden. Want to help?"

Emily looked doubtful. "Will there be bugs?"

"Probably, but they won't hurt you. What do you say?"

"I say no way," she said stubbornly. "The bugs are too buggy and the dirt's too dirty."

It was hard to argue with that. Fine—if that's the way Emily wanted to be, I was perfectly happy to have Aunt Hannah all to myself.

Using stakes and string, Aunt Hannah and I mapped out an area at the back of the yard for our garden. With the garden fork, Aunt Hannah dug up the grass and turned the soil over. I carried the clumps of grass and roots over to a back corner behind the garden shed, and then crumbled up the remaining clods with my hands while Aunt Hannah added shovelfuls of topsoil for me to rake smooth.

"Did you know that Massachusetts has a state soil to go with its state flower and state bird?" asked Aunt Hannah.

In third grade, we had learned the Massachusetts flower was the mayflower and the state bird was the black-capped chickadee. I even knew the state reptile, the garter snake. But a state *soil?* "I didn't even know soil had names," I said.

She smiled. "The Massachusetts state soil is named Paxton."

I whispered *Paxton* to myself, liking the way it sounded on my tongue. That was a cool factoid! I made a mental note to tell Dakota.

Mom came out the sliding door onto the deck. She and Emily peered over the railing at us, like meerkats who were suspicious about a change in their natural habitat.

"That's bigger than I thought it would be," Mom called to Aunt Hannah. "I hope you're remembering how much work a garden is to take care of."

"I'll help," I said quickly.

Aunt Hannah wiped her cheek with the back of her hand, leaving a dirty smudge. "It'll be worth all the work when we get to eat tomatoes that taste like sunshine and rain."

"Well, that's for sure," said Mom. "And I guess that if it gets to be too much, it's easy enough to turn it back into lawn." Mom draped her arm around Emily's shoulder. "Come on, Emily, let's help your dad get dinner started."

A puff of wind lifted my hair and cooled the back of my neck. A bird whistled in the tree over the driveway, and another one answered from across the yard.

"Sounds like you have whip-poor-wills here," said Aunt Hannah.

I looked at her in surprise. "You mean you can tell what they are just by how they chirp? Without even seeing the bird?"

My aunt nodded. "That's what I study, birdsongs. Would you like me to teach you how to do it?"

Would I ever! I nodded.

After a little more digging and raking, Aunt Hannah put down the fork and gazed at our new garden bed. "I call that pretty good work for one afternoon. Tomorrow we can set up the compost heap behind the garden shed, on top of the grass we dug up. We'll add fruit and vegetable scraps from your kitchen, and earthworms and bacteria will turn it into rich soil for our garden." She pointed to a corner of the house. "And right over there, we can put a rain barrel so that we won't have to use much city water on the garden. Your folks will like that."

I looked at our handiwork. Who knew that a black rectangle of dirt could feel so special? Maybe it was because of Aunt Hannah. Or maybe because it was *our* dirt—our special place for the food and flowers we would grow. "When do we start planting?" I asked.

"I'll pick up some seeds tomorrow while you're at school," Aunt Hannah said. "We can plant them in the afternoon when you get home."

Dinner was one of Dad's specialties from our pizza experiment: spaghetti pizza pie. You take cooked spaghetti noodles and spread them on the bottom of a pie pan. Then you spread on spaghetti sauce, and then cheese and toppings. When you take it out of the oven, it looks like deep-dish pizza, but it tastes like spaghetti. Dad had put kidney beans on it as one of the toppings, which seemed kind of strange. Angela thought so, too. She speared one on her fork and our eyes met across the table. I almost started giggling, but then I noticed Emily was eating it all happily, so I didn't laugh.

After dinner, Aunt Hannah and I couldn't resist going back outside. As the cool evening dropped around us, we lay on our backs in the grass and talked about dirt. I remarked that in a way, dirt is like a big shopping mall for plants because the roots go there to get food for the stems and leaves.

"Where does dirt come from?" I asked.

"Well," she said thoughtfully, "I believe most of the soils in New England were brought here by glaciers, giant sheets of ice that covered much of North America. When the glaciers melted, they left behind piles of rock and dirt. Some dirt was formed from rocks that got ground into tiny particles by the ice."

It was dark by now, and the first stars were out. The sky looked as if someone had taken a pin and poked it so teeny bursts of light could shine through.

"A friend of mine who studies astronomy tells

me there's a dark line of dust across the center of the Milky Way." Aunt Hannah lazily lifted her arm and traced the air with her finger. "And some of the elements here on earth can only have come from exploding stars."

"So we've been digging in stardust?"

"I guess we have." I could hear the smile in her voice.

The following night, I had news to send Dakota:

From: Lanie <hollandnotthecountry@4natr.net>
Date: April 21, 2010 8:07 P.M.
To: "Dakota" <dakotanotthestate@4natr.net>
Subject: Dirt is beautiful!
  Today I planted wildflower and vegetable seeds in our new backyard garden. I never knew boring old dirt could be so interesting. Did you know some scientists spend their whole lives studying dirt? (Except they call it soil.)
  There are all kinds of weird animals who live in

dirt--not just ants and earthworms, but also moles and grubs and beetles and even some kinds of bees. And once our wildflowers start blooming, they'll attract tons of insects, butter- flies, birds, and even bats. It'll be sort of like a miniature rain forest, full of life, right in my backyard. No orangutans, though! :-)

The next morning, I got up extra early and ran downstairs to admire our work from yesterday. But as soon as I reached the garden, something looked different. Our neatly planted rows were full of holes, diggings, and tiny paw prints.

Apparently my garden was already full of life. *Squirrel* life.

The squirrels must have thought we were laying out a feast just for them. They'd eaten a lot of the pea and sunflower seeds and had disturbed the soil— probably searching for other good stuff—in many of the rows. Total woe!

You'd think that cat next door could at least make himself useful chasing squirrels. Now what?

I sat back on my heels and looked glumly at our ruined garden. Two days ago, this was just our regular old ordinary backyard—a deck, a lawn, and a few trees. Pleasant enough, but nothing special. Somehow, planting a garden had transformed it. The squirrels hadn't exactly destroyed anything, because nothing had started growing yet, but I still felt angry and upset. Those stupid squirrels—how dare they?

Aunt Hannah came out of her trailer and crossed the lawn to gaze at the garden with me. "I see we've had visitors—hungry ones," she said, surveying the damage. "Guess we'll have to replant."

"If we plant again, all we'll get are fatter squirrels," I grumbled. "And here I used to think squirrels were cute! Now I know they're just a bunch of low-down, thieving trespassers."

Aunt Hannah smiled. "Actually, squirrels have lived in this area far longer than people. If anyone's a trespasser here, it's us. The squirrels are just looking for food. Think about it—it's springtime, so they're hungry after their long winter, and many of them probably have babies to feed." She put an arm around my shoulders. "Don't worry, Lanie. We'll outsmart those squirrels."

After school, I headed out to the backyard, with Emily tagging along behind me. On the table, Aunt Hannah was setting down a black tray filled with little plants. On the deck were about ten more trays, some with tiny matching plants and others with small pots holding larger plants.

"These plants will give the garden a head start," Aunt Hannah said. "But we'll still have to protect it from the critters." She held up a bottle labeled *Pest Away Pepper Spray*. "We'll spray this around the edge of the garden. That should stop most of the squirrels."

I had been thinking about those baby squirrels, and my attitude had softened a little. "Will it hurt them?"

"No, but they'll learn that if they try to invade or dig, they'll get red pepper on their feet, and they won't like that, so they'll stay away. And just to show them we mean no harm, I also got this." She held up a large wire contraption and gave it a spin. It looked like an open wheel with arms sticking out. At the end of each arm was a dried corncob. "The squirrels will prefer eating the corn we're going to put out for them and will leave our plants alone."

Emily looked fascinated. "Why does it spin? Is it to give the squirrels a ride?"

The Garden

"Yes!" Aunt Hannah grinned. "Squirrels are tons of fun to watch. We'll put it where you can see it from your deck."

"A squirrel Ferris wheel," Emily said, her eyes shining. "Let's put it up right now!"

After we'd nailed the squirrel feeder to the picket fence that ran along the back of the yard, Aunt Hannah and I started planting. Kneeling in the soil, we dug holes with our trowels, carefully slid each plant from its pot into the hole, and then patted the soil firm around it.

When we took a break, she showed me the picture on the front of a packet of wildflower seeds. Delicate flowers of all colors and shapes grew in graceful mounds in a meadow of tall waving grasses. The wildflowers looked natural, as if they had just grown that way by themselves without being planted by anyone. It was beautiful.

"Will our yard look like that?" I asked.

"Well, not right away. But in July, you'll start seeing some blossoms. By late summer, you should have a real show. And it'll get better every year." She set the seed packet down. "Once we've got the starter plants in the ground, we'll sprinkle these seeds in between to fill in the gaps. They're too small to interest the squirrels. Oh, and I got something I think you and Emily will especially like." She held up a slender green stick.

"What is it?" I asked.

"Milkweed cuttings!"

I tried not to look disappointed. Milkweed? Boring, messy old milkweed?

Aunt Hannah saw my face. "Well, we want butterflies in the garden, don't we? And I don't have to tell you that monarchs like milkweed."

"Do the grown-up butterflies like it, too?"

"Not to eat. They only sip nectar from flowers, and we'll have plenty of those. But the adult butterflies do need milkweed to lay their eggs on, since that's what their caterpillars eat. It's a coarse plant, but it's got an interesting blossom, and it'll look fine together with all the others."

I was sold. We'd plant milkweed in our wildflower garden and create a happy home for monarchs.

We worked all afternoon. By dinnertime, we had planted all the wildflowers. The trays of vegetables and herbs were still sitting on the deck waiting their turn. There was only one problem: the garden was out of space!

"Oh well, we'll just have to dig up more of the lawn to make a bed for the vegetable garden," Aunt Hannah said cheerfully. "It'll be closer to the kitchen that way, anyhow. Do you think your folks will mind?"

I shook my head. "I doubt it. Dad hates mowing the lawn. The less he has to mow, the happier he'll be."

We didn't get to start digging up the lawn for our vegetable garden right away, though, because the next day, Friday, it was raining. Instead, after school I hung out in Aunt Hannah's camper, learning how to identify birds from their songs.

"Birders use phrases to describe each call, almost like lyrics to a song," Aunt Hannah explained. "For example, black-capped chickadees say *hey sweetie.*" She sang out the phrase, whistled the notes, and then played the birdsong for me on her MP3 player.

It didn't exactly sound like the bird was talking, but when she sang the notes along with the words, I saw what she meant. "Cool. Let's do another one!"

I closed my eyes and concentrated as she played another birdcall, and another. I learned that common yellowthroats say *wichity wichity* and Carolina wrens say *tea kettle, tea kettle, tea kettle.* Then she showed me how her computer could turn the calls into pictures of sound waves.

I put a finger on the wavy lines on her monitor and felt a sense of awe. I was touching a bird's song!

"Each birdcall makes a unique pattern," Aunt Hannah explained. "By recording the birdsong in an area and then looking at the patterns from the recording, we can tell which birds were present, without actually having to see them with binoculars."

"But don't you *like* to see them?" I asked.

"Of course! If we can. But birds can be tricky to spot, so this is an identification technique we use for research." She peered out the window of her camper. "Looks like the rain is letting up. Come outside for a moment and I'll show you another thing you can do with recorded birdsong."

Aunt Hannah grabbed her MP3 player and a bird book, and I followed her into the backyard. She handed me the player's external speaker. "Hold this up high. I'm going to dial up a Carolina wren. Ready? We'll interrupt its life only briefly." She played the call.

Across the yard, a bird fluttered out of a bush. "There! Describe its markings," Aunt Hannah whispered.

"Rust-colored wings and yellow-white belly," I said softly. "Longish tail held upright. White eye stripe." I reached for her bird guidebook to see if that was what the Carolina wren looked like.

"Wait—watch as long as you can. Books don't fly away. Birds do."

Suddenly, the bird whistled out *tea kettle, tea kettle, tea kettle* as clear as anything. It had to be a Carolina wren! Aunt Hannah and I looked triumphantly at each other as she showed me the picture in the bird guide to confirm the sighting.

"In Massachusetts, the biggest bird show is in May. That's when most of the migratory birds are coming through New England, on their way from their warm winter homes to their summer nesting grounds in the north. I'll take you over to Mount Auburn Cemetery, and we'll see how many birds we can find. You'll love it."

Mount Auburn is just a few blocks away. "Could we bring this?" I held up the MP3 speaker.

"I'm glad you asked." She tapped me on my nose. "Dialing up a bird is a good tool to use on occasion, when you really need to locate a certain bird. But it's rude and disruptive to the bird—like calling someone to the door when no one's there. So we don't use it except in an emergency."

Now that the rain had stopped, other birds were joining the chorus. For a second I thought I heard the *wichity wichity* song Aunt Hannah had played for me in the trailer. I held my breath, listening, until it came again. "There! Wasn't that a common yellowthroat?" It was thrilling to recognize the call, even though I couldn't spot the bird itself.

Aunt Hannah grinned and nodded. "You've

obviously got the family's music gene, which definitely helps in identifying birdsongs."

I grinned back. "Like identifying the *William Tell Overture* as the song of the brown-haired sister bird?"

She laughed and grabbed me in a hug. I hugged her back. "You've probably heard wren calls almost as often as I've heard that song," I told her.

She gave me another squeeze. "Birdsong research is great, but it's way more fun sharing the birds with someone else," she said to the top of my head.

I knew exactly what she meant.

On Saturday, the ground was dry enough to work, so we got busy digging up more of the lawn. Not long after we started, a pickup truck pulled up in the driveway of the house next door. Soon Ms. Marshall came into her backyard with two young men, one pushing a wheelbarrow and the other carrying shovels and garden tools.

Ms. Marshall stepped onto her terrace and held up one of the boxes. I squinted, trying to get a closer look. It had spiky, thorny sticks poking out the top and a colorful picture on the side.

"There are thirty-six of them," she was saying. "Put eight in the front yard, on either side of the porch, and the rest in rows back here. Don't plant them too deep, because you'll be adding a heavy layer of mulch. And be sure to label each one correctly. Any questions?"

The young men shook their heads.

"Okay, then." She turned to leave, and then stopped. "And don't forget to add fertilizer—roses are heavy feeders." Then she went into the house.

Those spiky things were *roses*?

An hour later, she came back out to see how the men were doing. In the meantime, I had told Aunt Hannah all about the bunny walk and Lulu's attack on Caesar the cat. Somehow, as I was telling it to Aunt Hannah, it seemed sort of funny.

When Ms. Marshall was done talking to her gardeners, she looked over and saw us. Not wanting to be rude, I waved at her. To my surprise, she began walking toward us. When she reached the edge of her lawn, she hesitated, clearly concerned about walking in our freshly dug dirt. She carefully picked her way around it and came to where we were digging up the last of the lawn, except for the strip that ran in front of the deck and over to the driveway, where the camper was parked.

"Good morning. Beautiful day for gardening, isn't it?" She held out her hand to Aunt Hannah. "I'm Susan Marshall."

"I'm Hannah Wells, Lanie's aunt. It certainly is a great day for planting."

So far, so good. Maybe this would be a fresh start.

"I see you're taking out the lawn. What are you putting in?" Ms. Marshall asked.

"This area's for vegetables," my aunt told her.

"And that area over there has milkweed and other stuff that butterflies like," I added proudly.

Ms. Marshall was silent for a moment. "Milkweed?" she repeated, her eyebrows raised.

"Various native plants," Aunt Hannah explained. "It's a wild garden."

"It sounds more like a weed garden," Ms. Marshall said doubtfully. "Are you sure you know what you're doing?"

Aunt Hannah opened her mouth and then closed it again. I jumped in. "Of course we do!"

"Good, because I'd hate to get a lot of weed seeds blowing into my yard. This is my very first house and yard, and I want it to be beautiful. I'm having thirty-six prize-winning roses planted. It's quite an investment in my property. I—I didn't expect they'd be set against a backdrop of weeds."

"Wildflowers," Aunt Hannah corrected.

"And speaking of property values, may I ask how long you're planning to park that trailer here?"

"Just for the summer," Aunt Hannah replied mildly.

Ms. Marshall's expression went from doubtful to downright unhappy. "The whole summer?"

Aunt Hannah shrugged. "It's my home for the summer."

Now it was Ms. Marshall's turn to be speechless. Without another word, she turned and went back to her roses.

Aunt Hannah and I spent the rest of the day digging up lawn, smoothing soil lumps, and adding topsoil, just as we had for the wildflower garden. I kept an eye on the yard next door. The men planted the roses in evenly spaced rows with no other plants around them, just a thick layer of chopped-up bark. It seemed kind of boring to me, but when they were done, I had to admit that it all looked neat and tidy, whereas our yard was a muddy mess after all the rain and digging. Even the wildflowers we'd planted a few days ago looked limp and straggly compared to the sturdy, upright, orderly rosebushes. Still, they were so spiky, it was hard to imagine that they could ever be beautiful. But then our wildflowers didn't exactly look like the glorious picture on the seed packet, either.

"Well, I'm beat," Aunt Hannah said as we washed up for dinner. "We'll plant the veggies tomorrow."

The next morning, I woke up early and went out onto my bedroom deck. From above, the backyard looked strange: it was almost all dirt now, with just a small patch of lawn near the plum tree by the big deck, and a wide grass path to the back of the yard where the garden shed was. The vegetable flats were still arrayed on the deck, just waiting for us to plant them.

I hugged myself. Another day in the garden with Aunt Hannah! And tomorrow would be the start of spring break, so I could look forward to a whole week of fun outdoors with my aunt.

Still in my socks and pj's, I padded back inside and took a running slide across the smooth bamboo floors to my dresser. Our house has bamboo floors, a bamboo coffee table, and even bamboo sheets. Wait till someone invents a bamboo laptop—Mom will be first in line to buy it!

Factoid

Bamboo is the fastest growing plant on the planet, so it's a perfect renewable resource. Pandas love it—and so does my mom.

I got dressed and hurried downstairs. As I neared the first floor, I could see Mom and Dad in the kitchen, drinking coffee and reading the paper. This was highly unusual. It wasn't even seven A.M. yet, and they normally slept in on Sundays.

I burst into the room. "What's going on?"

Dad splashed coffee on his newspaper. "Lanie, you startled me! I think you just sent my brain into shock."

"Sorry. But why are you up so early?"

"Sweetie," Mom began, and then hesitated and exchanged a glance with Dad.

Uh-oh. A bad sign. Whatever it was, I didn't need to hear it. "I'm going to go see Aunt Hannah," I told them, heading to the deck door.

"Honey—she's gone," said Mom.

"Gone? What do you mean, gone? Her camper's right there."

"Just for six weeks," Mom explained. "She got a call last night from some bird people she knows in Costa Rica. One of the researchers on a project there broke his leg, and they asked her to fill in."

Six whole weeks? That was forever.

"I took her to the airport early this morning," Dad said. "She asked me to give you this." He handed me an envelope.

Inside it was the key to her camper and a letter:

Dear Lanie,
I'm going to be working on a very exciting project—recording bellbirds in Costa Rica! Can't wait to tell you all about it. Sorry I couldn't say good-bye—the call came after you were asleep.
Check the trailer for a surprise!
Love & hugs, Aunt Hannah

I put the note down. "I can't believe she's gone." What about all our plans for the backyard? And bird-watching together in Mount Auburn Cemetery? She had said the big bird show was in May—and now she would be gone for the whole month.

"We'll all miss her, but I know she was very pleased to be asked," said Mom. "It's an exciting opportunity for her."

I could tell Mom was trying to put a positive spin on things, but I was in no mood to hear it.

"They were just lucky Hannah had a passport and was willing to hop a plane right away," Dad said.

Yeah. Lucky for them.

Unlucky for me.

I ran outside and opened the camper. On the table was a pair of binoculars, the bird guide, a bag of corncobs, and another note.

> Lanie, don't forget to water the garden the way I showed you. If it rains, put on more pepper spray. Refill the squirrel feeder as needed. Use the guidebook and see how many birds you can identify! Some birders like to keep track of every bird they've ever spotted—a "Life List" of birds. Maybe you'll want to do that.   —Aunt Hannah
> P.S. I noticed your journal is almost full—here's a new one for you.

I sat there, looking around at the empty camper. The desk was tidy. A rinsed coffee mug sat in the sink.

The laptop and the MP3 player were gone.

Even with morning sunlight streaming in the windows, the camper just didn't seem as wonderful without Aunt Hannah in it.

Slowly, I went back inside the house. As I crossed the deck, I could barely look at the flats of baby vegetables sitting there. They were probably wondering who was going to plant them. I was wondering the same thing.

I trudged back up to my room to bring Lulu a handful of fresh grass, which was a treat for her. At least she was always there for me. At least she didn't go disappearing off to exotic countries at the drop of a hat to have incredible adventures with wild animals, leaving me stuck behind in boring old Boston. I picked her up and she snuffled her head into the crook of my elbow, her favorite spot. I buried my face in her sweet-smelling fur and told myself sternly that scientists don't cry.

After a few minutes, I decided to pour out my woes to Dakota. When my e-mail came up, as usual there was a message waiting for me.

> From: Dakota <dakotanotthestate@4natr.net>
> Date: April 24, 2010 6:52 P.M.
> To: Lanie <hollandnotthecountry@4natr.net>
> Subject: Fio and Teng
> Fio is doing a lot better. She's made a friend, and he protects her from the others. She's much happier now that she can hang with the group. She hated being all alone.

I knew just how Fio felt.

A few days ago the center got a new baby
orangutan named Teng. He's really tiny. He came
with his mother--the trees where they lived got
cut down, and she was so upset that she wasn't
taking care of him. While his mother rebuilds her
strength and adjusts to life at the center, Teng is
being bottle-fed. I got to help--check out the pix
of the orangutan nursery! In a month or 2, we
hope to release Teng and his mother back into the
forest.

Next week is our spring break, so we're going
camping in the rain forest with another family. I
wonder if we'll see any rare animals like a
Sumatran rhino or a sun bear? I'm bringing my
camera for sure!

How is your garden coming? It sounds
awesome. I love wildflowers. Send me a picture!

I opened the attachment. There was my best
friend, her arms full of the most adorable baby animal
I'd ever seen. He had huge brown eyes and wispy
orange hair, and his hand gripped Dakota's finger. In
the next picture, she was feeding him from a baby
bottle. The last picture showed a small room with six
baskets, each holding blankets and one or two baby

orangutans. Dakota and a few other kids stood grinning beside a young Indonesian woman who was dressed sort of like a park ranger.

Strange feelings began swirling inside of me. My stomach felt like a bubbling mud pot. In fact, it was as if I had a volcano inside me, bubbling furiously, about to explode.

Before I could even think, I hit the reply button and started typing:

> From: Lanie <hollandnotthecountry@4natr.net>
> Date: April 25, 2010 7:38 A.M.
> To: Dakota <dakotanotthestate@4natr.net>
> Subject: Re: Fio and Teng
>   I'm very happy that you and your new friends get to play with baby orangutans and feed them and everything. That must be so great. I can hardly imagine how great it must be. In fact, I don't even want to imagine it, so don't send me any more pictures. Okay?

My door swung open and Emily peeked in, accompanied by the familiar notes of the *William Tell* Overture. Hadn't Angela mastered that song yet? Wasn't it time for her to learn a new one? Or was she just trying to torture me?

Emily barged into my room. "Hey Lanie, Mom's making pineapple pancakes—she told me to tell you they'll be ready in a few minutes. Aunt Hannah left, but she's coming back. Hey, can I play with Lulu while we're waiting for the pancakes to be ready?"

"No! And stay out of my room." I jumped up and slammed the door, then returned to my computer.

> My sisters are driving me crazy. Nobody in my family understands me. Except for my aunt, and she just left for Costa Rica. There's no point in sending you a picture of my garden, because so far it just looks like a bunch of dirt.

That was all the news I had, so I hit the send button.

After breakfast, I moped in my room for a while and then decided to take Lulu outside. I put on her walking vest and carried her down the street a ways, in the opposite direction from Ms. Marshall's house. Lulu seemed happy to be outside and did great again on the leash, but I no longer felt any sense of triumph. The volcanic goo was still inside me, simmering.

Eruption

I came home and tied Lulu to the plum tree by the deck while I got out the hose to water the wildflower plants. They looked small and pathetic. I tried to remind myself of the beautiful wild garden pictured on the seed packet, but I could hardly remember what it looked like.

Before winding the hose back up, I took it over to the deck and gave the vegetable flats a few squirts. To my surprise, even though it had rained a few days ago, the soil in the flats was already bone-dry. Some of the baby vegetables looked top-heavy and ready to flop over, as though they were already too big for their tiny pots. It was obvious that they needed to get into the ground as soon as possible.

But there were so many of them! Each flat had eighteen plants, and there were three flats of tomatoes, zucchini, peppers, and herbs—that made fifty-four plants. If they didn't get planted, and soon, they would die. I couldn't let that happen. What would I tell Aunt Hannah? I wasn't going to abandon her baby plants the way she had abandoned me—yet how could I possibly plant them all myself?

I fetched a trowel from the garden shed and started digging holes. At least the small plants didn't need very big holes. Still, it was slow going working alone, and my mood didn't improve, even after Mom came out with a sandwich and some lemonade.

"Wow, Lanie, that's a lot of hard work you're doing. Aunt Hannah will be very impressed when she gets back."

Emily was sitting in the hammock on the deck watching us. Suddenly she spoke up. "I can do hard work, too. Wanna see?"

"Sure! Are you going to help Lanie in the garden?" Mom asked Emily.

"No way," said Emily. "But I helped her with her field notes." She glanced quickly at me and then gave Mom her winning, gap-toothed smile.

My heart skipped a beat, and I put down my trowel. "What do you mean, Emily?"

She wouldn't look at me, just smiled up at Mom, who beamed back at her, obviously without a clue that something serious might have happened. "The cater-pillars are all turned into butterflies," Emily replied in a singsong voice, swinging the hammock with her legs.

"Emily—what are you talking about?" Pulling off my gardening gloves, I stepped up onto the deck. I went over to the hammock and glared down at her. "Where's my journal?"

Slowly Emily lifted up her shirt. There was my

science journal, sitting on her bare tummy. I reached for it, but she quickly handed it to Mom. "See? I'm a scientist too."

Mom glanced at me, and then began paging through the journal. I watched, frozen to the spot, as she turned past my pictures of Stripey, my meerkat sketches, and my caterpillars hanging in J's. That was the last entry I had made. Mom turned the page, and there, in brightly colored crayon, were lumpy, lime-green pupas. On the next page—the last one in the journal—were big black and orange butterflies with long black antennas and six carefully drawn legs. Each butterfly had a smiling face.

My face was not smiling. More like scowling with fury. I snatched the journal from Mom and stared at it in disbelief. "Emily, this was my journal for science class, and you knew that! These were my field notes, and I worked really hard on them, and now you've ruined them. You've ruined the whole book!"

Emily had been looking up at me fearfully, and now she burst into tears. "I just wanted to make the butterflies," she sobbed. "I want to be a scientist like you and Aunt Hannah!"

Mom took Emily into her arms. "Lanie, that's a little extreme. She didn't ruin the whole book. It looks like she just colored on the last few pages. I'm sure your teacher will understand."

The volcano inside me erupted. "That's not the point! This was my work, my scientific observations. She had no right to draw in my journal—"

Mom nodded. "I know, Lanie, but she obviously wants—"

"If she wants to be a scientist so badly, then she has to stop being such a fraidycat about bugs!" I was tempted to add, *She'll never be a scientist—she has inside genes, just like the rest of you.*

Instead I kicked off my mud-caked shoes and headed for my room. As I climbed the stairs, the *William Tell* Overture floated down to greet me.

Before I could think, I burst into Angela's room. "Don't you know any other songs?" I shouted.

The sudden silence was shocking.

Angela put down the bow. "Wow, Lanie. Are you okay? I heard about Aunt Hannah leaving." She said it with such sympathy, I felt like howling.

I slumped onto her bed and everything came spilling out, about how Dakota and Aunt Hannah were having amazing adventures while I was left behind to make field notes on fourth-graders and caterpillars, only to have them ruined by Emily. How Dakota had

Eruption

Indonesia and Aunt Hannah had Costa Rica, and all I had was the backyard.

Angela picked up her hairbrush and came over. She sat down next to me on the bed and started working on my hair. "You know, I've been watching from my deck, and it looks like you're doing some amazing things in the backyard. The squirrels are so cute on that new feeder—I'm really glad you put that up. I love watching them."

I sighed and slumped forward as she brushed my hair. It was nice of her to try to make me feel better, but I knew she couldn't possibly understand how I felt.

"Lanie, everyone knows about my dream of becoming a concert cellist," she said, "but you have dreams, too, don't you." I nodded, and Angela gave my shoulders a squeeze. "Here's something my cello teacher always tells me: the secret to achieving a big dream is to keep taking small steps, and don't let setbacks stop you."

She pulled on a snarl, and then paused to pick it apart with her fingers. "Here's another secret that I've never told anyone: sometimes I get really tired of practicing cello."

I sat up. "Seriously?"

She nodded. "You think *you're* tired of the

William Tell Overture? Sometimes I think if I have to play it one more time, I'll scream!" She chuckled, and I felt a surprised smile poking at my mouth. "But then when I play it perfectly, suddenly it sounds beautiful again, and I know I've become a better musician—and I'm that much closer to achieving my dream." She ran the brush smoothly through my hair. "Small steps, Lanie, lots and lots of them—that's what it takes."

Suddenly I realized I'd left Lulu tied to the plum tree. "Thanks, Angela—and thanks for doing my hair," I mumbled, and hurried downstairs.

Mom and Emily had left the deck. As I untied Lulu, I heard a familiar sound—*tea kettle tea kettle tea kettle!*—coming from the area near the garden shed. A Carolina wren. The call was so easy to recognize now that I knew it. I squinted and peered out across the yard, trying to spot the bird, but I couldn't see it. Slowly I began walking toward the shed . . .

> . . . *I'm deep in a mountain forest, searching for rare tropical birds. Vines hang from the trees, and the jungle canopy arches overhead, thick and green and leafy. Mysterious noises surround me—the cry of howler monkeys, the call of bellbirds, the rush of a great waterfall nearby . . .*

Tea kettle tea kettle tea kettle. I blinked and shook my head. Where *was* that little wren hiding?

I looked up into the branches overhead. The wren was nowhere to be seen, but the plum tree's new leaves shimmered and glowed in the sunlight. All around me, warm earthy smells rose from the newly turned soil. Birdsong rang cheerfully back and forth between our yard and the neighbors'.

Even though I still couldn't spot the wren, suddenly I felt strangely grateful to it. In searching for it, I had discovered something else.

Maybe I wasn't in the Costa Rican jungle or the Indonesian rain forest, but my backyard was still full of beauty and mystery and things to explore.

Maybe I could have an adventure right here in my own backyard.

"And here's a flashlight," Mom said, handing it to me. "Now, I'll leave the deck door unlocked, and if you get too cold, you can just come back inside."

I nodded and added the flashlight to my backpack of supplies, which included a sleeping bag, a tarp, a pillow, a water bottle, and a guide to constellations, even though in Boston the sky isn't dark enough to see very many stars.

I was about to start Real Adventures, Step One.

Dad handed me a little bundle wrapped in foil. "Here's the last of the chocolate. Just in case you need some sustenance."

"Thanks, Dad." I slipped the bundle into my pack.

Emily hung back but didn't take her eyes off me. We had hardly spoken during dinner. I was still mad at her, although in a private moment Mom had pulled me aside, saying, "Remember, imitation is the sincerest form of flattery."

"What's that supposed to mean?" I asked.

"It means Emily looks up to you. It's a big responsibility, being a big sister." I still wasn't sure what she was talking about, but I had nodded as if I under-stood, eager to get outside and begin my adventure.

Now that it was really happening, I suddenly felt a bit nervous. I spread out my tarp, laid my pillow and sleeping bag on top of it, and climbed in, pretending I was a chimpanzee settling into my nest. At first it was a fun, cozy feeling. Then being a chimp made me think of Dakota and the orangutans, and I remembered the last e-mail I had sent. Would Dakota still want to be my friend after she read it?

Pushing the thought out of my mind, I lay back and looked up at the stars.

Hey, was that the Big Dipper?

I unzipped my backpack, pulled out my star guide, and flipped on the flashlight. Yes! The pattern shown in the book was a perfect match for the stars shining above me.

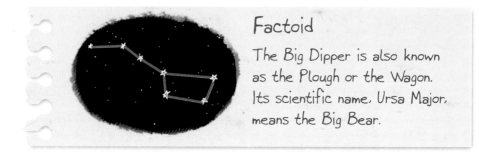

Factoid

The Big Dipper is also known as the Plough or the Wagon. Its scientific name, Ursa Major, means the Big Bear.

I thought again about the fact that the soil I was lying on had once been part of a star, billions of years ago.

It made me feel very small and insignificant, but also strangely excited to be part of something so vast— not just the wide wonderful world, but the whole universe.

The next morning I woke up very early to a chorus of birdsong. A heavy layer of dew lay on my sleeping bag, but inside I was toasty warm. My pillow was damp, though, too. I could see why people preferred camping in tents or campers. Still, it was thrilling to open my eyes and be outside already, looking up at the trees. I heard a little noise—a squirrel was doing gymnastics on the feeder, making it spin as he tried to get to a corn-cob. Angela was right—the squirrels really were cute. I wondered if Emily had seen them yet. She might be afraid of bugs, but she loves small furry animals.

I tiptoed inside. Nobody was up yet. I padded up to Emily's room and went in. She opened her eyes and looked at me.

"Come here—I want to show you something," I told her, taking her hand. She slipped out of bed and followed me out to her little bedroom deck. It's on the second floor, not as high as mine, so we had a closer view of the yard. I pointed down at the squirrel feeder. The squirrel was doing crazy ninja moves, jumping from cob to cob and making the feeder spin.

Emily watched for a few moments and then turned to me. "I think he needs more corn."

I squinted at the feeder. Now that she pointed it out, the corncobs did look sort of white and chewed over. "That's a very good observation, Emily. I think you're right." Suddenly an idea flapped by, and I caught it. Maybe I didn't have to be alone. Maybe I could convince Emily to help me with the backyard. "Hey, Aunt Hannah left us a bag of corncobs for refills. You want to help refill the squirrel feeder?"

She nodded solemnly.

After helping Emily put new cobs on the feeder, I hung my damp sleeping bag and the tarp over the deck railing to dry. Emily was still standing near the feeder, calling the squirrel, who was scolding her from a tall tree, to come and try his new corn. So far she hadn't said one word about bugs. *Small steps.* Maybe I could try another one.

"Emily, you know Stripey? Well, come take a look over here." I led her over to the wildflower area and squatted down beside a plant. "Recognize this?" Emily shook her head. "It's milkweed. What Stripey eats. Or used to eat, before he became a pupa."

Emily frowned. "That's not milkweed. It's just a stick."

"Well, it's a cutting—it has to grow more. And it will." I tried to sound confident. "And then we'll get some monarch butterflies right here in our backyard!"

I thought I saw a flicker of interest in Emily's

eyes as she gazed around at the wildflower-garden-to-be. Suddenly she pointed. "What's that?"

Something was moving in the grass by the garden shed. Brown wings, yellow chest, upright tail—it was a Carolina wren, maybe the one I'd heard last night. It was hopping along the ground carrying a twig in its mouth. As Emily and I watched, it hopped over to an old boot lying by a corner of the shed and tried to put the twig in the boot. The twig was too long, but the wren gave it several determined pushes, and finally, just when I figured the bird would give up, it found a way to push the twig in lengthwise. Then it hopped onto the boot and sang a loud, bubbling song.

We watched as the wren went after more twigs, stopping every so often to sing or rearrange them. I squeezed Emily's hand. "She's making a nest—maybe we'll be able to watch her lay eggs and raise babies! Come on, let's go check the bird book and see what it says."

We ran along the dewy grass path back to the house. Emily peered over my shoulder as I showed her the picture of the wren in the bird guide. "Oh—it says only the male wren sings," I told her. "And it's the male that builds the nest, so I guess the one we saw was a male. Listen to this—he builds a bunch of nests, and the female gets to pick the one she likes."

"I hope she picks the boot one," said Emily. "I'd like it if I were a bird."

I smiled at her. "Me too."

Emily picked up the bird book and started flipping through it. "Wow, look at all these birds! Will they come to our yard, too?"

"Well, no, probably most of them won't," I told her, and she looked disappointed.

The last thing I wanted was to discourage her newfound interest in birds. Then I remembered something Aunt Hannah had said. "Hey, I know of a place where we might be able to see some more birds right now. Go get dressed, and meet me down here in ten minutes."

I ran up to my room and pulled on some clothes. Then I went back downstairs, checked in with Mom and Dad, and threw some muffins into my backpack, along with the bird book and the binoculars. Ten minutes later, Emily and I were on our way out the door.

"Where are we going?" she asked me after we'd walked a little ways.

"Bird-watching," I said, handing her a muffin as

we turned the corner. At the end of the next block we crossed the street and entered Mount Auburn Cemetery.

Even though it was only about seven in the morning, we weren't alone. In fact, we were practically part of a parade. All along the path, little groups of people were staring into branches, peering through binoculars, and pointing. Emily and I looked into the branches as we passed a few groups, but we couldn't see anything. Finally the path was blocked by a crowd of people gazing up into a tree, and we had to stop.

"What is it?" I whispered to a teenage girl who was staring through a small pair of binoculars.

Her binoculars didn't budge. "A scarlet tanager."

I got my binoculars up and looked where the girl was looking. Suddenly, a blazing red bird with shiny black wings was right there in my lenses. "Ooh-la-la," I breathed.

"Let me see!" whispered Emily.

I handed her the binoculars. "Right there—see if you can spot it."

At first, Emily had trouble aiming the binoculars, but suddenly she let out a gasp and an "Ooooh!" and I knew she had found the tanager.

When the spot got too crowded,

we moved on. "What are you on?" I heard over and over—a bird-watcher's way of asking what someone was looking at. The answers were like another language: Yellow-rumped warbler. Cedar waxwing. Baltimore oriole. Common grackle. Half the time Emily and I couldn't find the birds, but I was thrilled to recognize the call of the common yellowthroat—*wichity wichity*— even though I couldn't spot the bird itself. Suddenly I heard another familiar sound—*tea kettle, tea kettle, tea kettle*.

"Emily—look for a Carolina wren! Just like the bird we saw building the nest in the boot."

She turned her binoculars toward the sound, searched for a moment, and then fixed them on a point.

"Do you see it?" I asked.

"I see something, but it's not like the one in our yard."

"Are you sure?"

She nodded and handed me the binoculars. "Its tail is a lot longer, and it's a different color."

I looked where she was pointing. She was right. This bird was all gray and about twice the size of the wren. It made the *tea kettle* call several more times, and then burst into a completely different song. What on earth was it?

I gave the binoculars back to Emily and got out the bird book. It took me a little while, but I finally located the bird.

"Emily, it's a northern mockingbird! Listen to this: 'The mockingbird mimics other birdcalls perfectly and has even been known to mimic a barking dog or a siren.' Isn't that crazy?"

Emily nodded, her eyes round.

Part of me wanted to stay at Mount Auburn all day and keep discovering new birds. But another part of me couldn't wait to get back home and start on my new journal from Aunt Hannah, making field notes and drawings of everything we'd seen. And now I had a whole bunch of birds to add to my Life List.

When it came to watching wildlife, maybe Boston wasn't so boring after all.

Emily and I were starving when we got home.

"You're just in time for tuna-fish pizza!" Dad announced. He placed a round of pita bread with tuna salad spread on it and cheese melted on top in front of Emily. Then he served Angela and me normal tuna-melt sandwiches on regular bread.

"Where's Mom?" I asked.

"She had to meet a client," said Dad.

I sighed. I'd been hoping that maybe I could get her to help me plant the rest of the vegetable garden this afternoon.

"What's your favorite kind of pizza?" Emily asked Angela.

Dad and I looked at each other. Our secret pizza experiment had been successful so far—we didn't want Angela to ruin it by revealing that some of Dad's inventions weren't really, truly pizza. I tried to signal her but couldn't catch her eye.

"Pizza? Well, I like the regular kind—you know, with tomato sauce and cheese and pepperoni," said Angela.

"That's my favorite kind, too," said Emily. She turned to Dad. "How come we don't have the regular kind more often? You can buy pizza at the store, you know. Then you just take it right out of the package and put it in the oven. That's how my friend Sophie's mother does it. I watched her, and it's really easy. It'll save you work."

I looked at Dad, wondering how he was going to answer her. He doesn't like using what he calls "convenience foods"—he always says homemade foods are much healthier. And here we'd worked so hard to convince Emily that pizza came in all different flavors, even tuna fish, so that she would eat a balanced diet. If she started insisting on store-bought frozen pizza, it would be a problem.

"Well, Emily, I suppose perhaps we could do that once in a while, but . . ." As Dad hesitated, another idea flapped by and flew right into my brain.

"Hey, Dad—what if we had fresh pizza ingredients like tomatoes and peppers and spices growing right in our backyard?"

He turned to me. "Well, that's certainly a nice idea, but since we don't—" He broke off and glanced outside at the dug-up yard. "Do we?"

I grinned. "We will! As soon as we finish planting the stuff Aunt Hannah bought." I turned to Emily. "Let's do it right after lunch. Just wait till we tell Aunt Hannah that you and I planted a pizza garden. She'll be so impressed!"

"Hey, I'll help with that," Dad offered. "Angela, are you in?"

"No way," she said with a toss of her head. "But I'll do the lunch cleanup so that you pizza farmers can get to work."

Since it was supposed to be a pizza garden, Emily asked if we could plant it in a circle, to look like a pizza.

"Great idea, Emily," said Dad. "A circle will be easier to mow around, too." He rubbed his hands together. "Just think of all those yummy fresh veggies to cook with!"

By late afternoon, we were done. I felt very relieved to get every last little plant into the ground. Dad headed back inside, and I showed Emily how to water the baby plants gently.

Emily took the hose. "When I'm done watering, let's go look around the yard and see if we can find anything interesting," she suggested.

I blinked at her. Maybe my little sister did have some outside genes after all. I mean, here was scientific evidence: All day, she hadn't complained once about dirt or bugs. And she had spent the entire day with me—outside. I grinned at Emily. "Wow, are you an alien? What have you done with my sister?" I joked, and she giggled. Then I helped her put away the hose, and we began walking around the yard to see what we could see.

The first thing we saw wasn't wildlife—it was Caesar, Ms. Marshall's orange cat, slinking across the neighbor's lawn and into our yard. When he got to the edge of the wildflower area, he paused at the bare dirt, sniffed it, and then zipped across, making a beeline for the garden shed.

"Here, kitty, kitty," called Emily. She's never met a furry animal she doesn't like. But I still hadn't forgiven Caesar for giving Lulu a bad name, and I didn't like the idea of him creeping around our yard threatening birds and squirrels.

I was about to shoo him out when I saw Ms. Marshall coming across her lawn calling, "Caesar! Come on back here." She stopped and frowned when she noticed Emily and me, and opened her mouth as if she was about to say something. I braced myself— somehow every conversation with her seemed to end badly. Then I noticed her gaze sliding up over my head, and her frown melted into a look of wonder.

Pizza

"Oh my, that's the first one I've seen here," she murmured. I followed where she was staring. There, fluttering in the air not far from us, was a monarch butterfly.

"Look, Emily," I said. "Look!" The three of us stood absolutely still until it was gone.

Very slowly, Ms. Marshall let out her breath. "My grandmother and I used to sit in her rose garden every year in May, watching for the first monarch."

This was my chance to explain to her about our wildflower garden. "Monarchs need milkweed," I began. No, that wasn't quite right. "I mean, their caterpillars do, so the monarchs have to lay their eggs—" A movement caught my eye.

The cat. Creeping toward the garden shed . . . the boot—

Emily shrieked.

"Shoo!" I hollered, waving my arms. Caesar yowled and streaked back to his own yard, with his owner hurrying after him.

I sighed. Just when we almost had her on our side.

That night I logged on to my e-mail, hoping—for the first time ever—that there *wouldn't* be a message from Dakota waiting for me.

There wasn't.

Of course, that could mean one of two things: either Dakota was still on her camping trip and hadn't seen my volcanic e-mail eruption, or else she had seen it and was so mad at me, she didn't want to be my friend anymore.

I really, really hoped it was the first one.

> From: Lanie <hollandnotthecountry@4natr.net>
> Date: April 26, 2010 7:38 P.M.
> To: Dakota <dakotanotthestate@4natr.net>
> Subject: Bears and aliens
> Hey! Did you have an awesome camping trip? Guess what--so did I! I slept out in my backyard. So, did you see any rhinos or bears when you were camping? I did--I saw a big bear, right from my backyard. Seriously! (Hint: its scientific name is Ursa Major. Get it? :-)
> If you haven't read the last e-mail I sent you yet, do me a big favor--delete it without reading it. If you already read it, please just delete it from your brain, OK? Aliens took over my body and made me write it.
> Seriously, I had a bad day but I'm doing better now.

Pizza

How is Teng? Will he and his mother be able to
return to the forest? Send me all the orangutan
news!
   Miss u tons,
   xoxo Lanie

This had to be the first time in my life that I couldn't wait to go back to school after spring break. Emily and I arrived early and hurried to Emily's classroom. Fortunately, since the caterpillars had all started becoming pupas just before break, they hadn't needed any milkweed deliveries. Now it was time for them to start hatching into butterflies.

Emily and I looked into the terrarium. The pupas were still hanging, but they had changed. They had lost their bright green color and had become almost clear. You could even sort of see the butterflies folded up inside.

Mrs. Kaminsky showed us that two of the pupas were too close together. She explained that if a butterfly comes out and has to lean against anything, its wings can dry crumpled, and then it won't be able to fly right. Mrs. Kaminsky told me to reach in and put my hand under the pupa while she cut the silk thread that it was hanging from. She put a dot of white glue on a stick, and I held the pupa in its new place until the glue set.

"Good," said Mrs. Kaminsky. "They're going to start hatching any day now."

Emily hung at my elbow. "Ooh! See the butterfly inside, Lanie? I can see its wings—can you? Are you going to put it in your field notes?"

"Wait and see," I told Emily. "Today, after school, I'll show you a field-note surprise."

As soon as we got home that afternoon, I made Emily wait in her room while I got things ready. She kept calling, "Is it time yet?" Finally, I led her out to the deck. There, on the table, was my new journal from Aunt Hannah. Beside it were the bird guidebook and my colored pencils from school.

Emily put her hands behind her. I could tell she wanted to touch things but knew she shouldn't.

"Go ahead—open it." I pointed to the journal.

Carefully, she opened the cover. There, on the first page, I had written:

OUR BACKYARD
by Lanie and Emily Holland

Emily looked up at me, a question on her face.

"Want to be my assistant?" I asked. "We'll make field notes on all the birds and butterflies we see in our backyard."

"Squirrels too?"

"Squirrels too." I smiled. "Let's start with the monarch we saw here the other day. We can draw a picture of the monarch's life cycle, from egg to butterfly. I'll draw the caterpillar. Do you want the pink and green pencils, for the milkweed? Or the orange and black, for the butterfly?"

"Really?" She looked at me with big eyes. "I can use your colored pencils?"

I nodded. "Really."

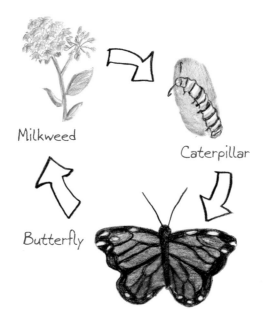

Milkweed

Caterpillar

Butterfly

Tuesday morning, as soon as Emily and I entered the school, Mrs. Kaminsky met us in the hall. "I'm so glad you girls are here early. Come on, hurry!" She led us to the terrarium. Emily and I gasped.

One butterfly was already out, perched on a stick. As we watched, a second chrysalis split open, and a crumpled-looking butterfly crawled out.

"Eww—it looks all weird," said Emily.

The butterfly's wings were wrinkled and small, and its body was much fatter than the other butterfly's body. It looked sort of like a caterpillar with messy wings. "Is there something wrong with it?" I asked.

Mrs. Kaminsky shook her head. "It will pump fluid from its body to its wings. The wings will get bigger and its body will get thinner. The wings have to dry, too."

The bell rang. Kids started pushing in, crowding around to watch as another butterfly came out.

"After school, we'll release the butterflies that have hatched," said Mrs. Kaminsky. "You're welcome to stay and help."

That afternoon, the monarchs rose into the air one by one and flew for the very first time, their crisp

wings brilliant orange against the blue sky. Watching them, I suddenly felt breathless with eagerness and joy. Soon, my very own backyard would be full of monarchs, sipping nectar from our wildflowers and laying eggs on our milkweed. I could hardly wait. Just think—there were magical, miraculous creatures right in my own backyard, and I never even knew it.

I looked at Emily, who was gazing in wonder as the monarchs' new wings lifted them into the air, and it struck me: in a way, Emily herself had new wings— and in a way I guess I did, too. Like the butterflies, we had changed—and in the process, we had discovered a wider, more wonderful world right around us.

As the butterflies fluttered up and away, I sent good thoughts spinning to Dakota and the orangutans on the other side of the world.

When we got home, Emily and I went straight into the backyard to check the boot and look for the monarch. We couldn't find the butterfly, but as we got near the shed, we could see something rustling by the boot. It was a wren, perched on the edge of the boot. It didn't sing, just scolded when we came too close.

"I think that's the female," I said. "Remember what the book said? The female doesn't sing, but she decides if she likes the nest or not."

"I think she likes it!" said Emily.

"It looks like she does, but I'm not sure it would be safe. I think we'd better put the boot up."

"Because of the cat?"

I nodded. "Don't worry—remember, the book said the male wren builds several nests, so she has others to choose from."

After moving the boot onto a shelf inside the garden shed, we wandered around the yard looking for the monarch, but it was nowhere to be found.

"It was an early butterfly—it's probably still on its way north," I told Emily. "Plus it needs milkweed to lay its eggs on, and our milkweed is still small. By the time Aunt Hannah gets back, our milkweed will be nice and big. Then we'll get some more monarchs, I bet."

Emily took my hand. "When Aunt Hannah comes back, will you still do stuff with me?"

"Definitely." I squeezed her hand. "It's way more fun now that you're in the backyard with me."

Wings

After I finished my homework, I checked my e-mail. Sure enough, one was waiting for me. A little nervously, I opened it.

From: Dakota <dakotanotthestate@4natr.net>
Date: May 2, 2010 5:45 P.M.
To: Lanie <hollandnotthecountry@4natr.net>
Subject: Re: Bears and Aliens
   Don't worry, Lanie--we all have our bad days. Even the orangutans get crabby sometimes. They act really mean and bare their teeth. But they don't scare me, and neither do you!
   We only have 5 more weeks of school, & then I'll be coming home!!! I know I'll really miss the orangutans, but here's an idea: if you have another bad day, you can just hang around with me and act like a crabby orangutan, and then I won't miss them as much! ;-)

I smiled. Dakota is the best. I quickly sent her a reply telling her about the monarchs, and then went downstairs to dinner.

As we sat down to eat, Dad picked up his water glass and cleared his throat. "Today I mowed the lawn, and it only took me a total of twenty minutes—fifteen in the front yard and a mere five in the back. That left me extra time to watch those silly squirrels spinning on their feeder, which was certainly far more enjoyable than mowing. All in all, I must say, our backyard has never looked more . . . interesting. A toast to Lanie and Emily!"

"Hear, hear," Mom said. Angela raised her water glass and clinked it with Mom's.

Dad continued. "And now, I'd like to make a proposal. Watching Lanie and Emily and Aunt Hannah transform the backyard has convinced me it's time for this family to try another camping trip."

We all stared at him.

He grinned. "Maybe I can figure out how not to break my other ankle."

Angela slowly lowered her water glass, landing it on the table with a little clunk. "On one condition." She paused dramatically. "If I can bring my cello."

Everyone looked at me.

That wasn't exactly how I had pictured it. I had imagined us roughing it in a tent. But maybe if we waited until Aunt Hannah returned, and if she brought her camper. . . . I decided it was time for me to be generous with the people in my family who were stuck with their inside genes.

"Sure," I said. "Why not?"

Letter from American Girl

Dear Readers,

Every year we receive thousands of letters from girls. Many of these letters are about concern for animals and the environment. Some girls ask for ideas on how to be earth-friendly. Others write to share what they are doing to help endangered species.

A good way to start is by getting to know the plants and animals around you. Like Lanie, you could plant a garden that will harbor butter-flies, birds, and other wildlife. Or, like Dakota, you could learn all about an endangered species and the challenges it faces. There are many ways to help—the important thing is to get started!

From recycling to organic gardening to raising money for endangered animals, every girl can find a way to make a difference.

Your friends at American Girl

GROWING A GARDEN

Dear American Girl,
Two of my friends at school are talking about how their parents are part of a community garden, where they grow flowers and vegetables. It sounds like fun, but I don't live anywhere near them. I'd like to try it in our backyard, but don't know where to start.
—Garden Girl

Ask your parents if you can use part of your yard for a garden. Gardening is fun, but it can be a lot of work, so start with just a few plants. Next, figure out how much sun your garden area gets, and choose plants that will grow in those conditions. Most vegetables need at least a half day of sun. Be sure to leave enough room between the baby plants for them to grow to their full size, and try to use some kind of mulch around the base of each plant to keep moisture in and weeds out. If you stick with it and keep your garden watered and weeded, you'll soon have your own homegrown food and flowers to enjoy.

HOW CAN I HELP?

Dear American Girl,
I really want to help endangered tigers, but I'm not sure how to go about doing it. What can I do to help them?
—Curious

Start by raising awareness. Many people don't realize tigers are endangered—you can help by spreading the word, perhaps in a school report or science fair project, or just in casual conversation. You can also raise money to help tiger research and preservation. Maybe you can start a save-the-tigers club by working with other kids who love tigers as much as you do.

Talk to a teacher about starting a school club, or to a scout leader or another adult about doing something outside of school. See the Web sites on page 107 for more ideas. Working with other people in a club or fund-raising effort is a great way to spread the word and make a difference.

GOING TO WASTE

Dear AG,
Every December a place in my town sells Christmas trees. They have so many left over after the holidays! Every time I drive by and see all of the beautiful trees that will go to waste, I feel like crying. What can I do?
—Want to Help

It might make you feel a little better to know that many cities and communities grind up old Christmas trees to make wood chips for gardens and paths, so the trees do get used again. And Christmas trees are planted and harvested on tree farms, as a crop; forests are not destroyed when Christmas trees are cut. After the holidays, you can put your Christmas tree in your yard, where it will provide shelter for winter birds and other animals.

It's great that you're sensitive to the issue of waste. It's important for each of us to think carefully about how to get the most use out of the things we buy.

DREAMS

Dear AG,
My friend and I want to be professional wildlife photographers, but we feel discouraged because our family and friends say we can't.
—Discouraged Dreamers

Of course you can achieve this dream—nature magazines, books, calendars, and TV shows all need wildlife photographers! Start by learning as much about this career as you can. Collect nature photos you love and write down what you like about each one—the animal's expression, the colors and lighting, or the angle of the shot. Take interesting photos of the animals around you—backyard birds and household pets count! Take shots of flowers and plants, too. Share your photos with your friends and talk about them. Keep learning and practicing, and you'll both make good progress toward achieving your dreams.

HOW I HELPED

Dear AG,

I did something special for my birthday and Christmas, and I think it's a great idea for other girls to do, too. Instead of presents, I asked for money to support animal conservation through the World Wildlife Fund. They have something called Panda Pages, through which I raised and donated money. Basically, you create your own Web site and you can put lots of stuff on it. So far, I've raised $330 between my birthday and Christmas.

I also "adopted" animals and through that made $150, for a total of $480 to help animals. I hope to donate at least $1,000 within a few years. I believe that if we all really try our hardest to conserve what is left of our world, we can save many animals and plants.
—Making a Difference